Pet-sitters
Plus Five

Pet-sitters Plus Five

by Tricia Springstubb

Illustrated by Nancy Poydar

A
LITTLE APPLE
PAPERBACK

SCHOLASTIC INC.
New York Toronto London Auckland Sydney

ISBN 0-590-46127-3

Copyright © 1993 by Tricia Springstubb
Illustrations copyright © 1993 by Scholastic Inc.
All rights reserved. Published by Scholastic Inc.
APPLE PAPERBACKS is a registered trademark of Scholastic Inc.

12 11 10 9 8 7 6 5 4 3 2 1   3 4 5 6 7 8/9

Printed in the U.S.A.   28

First Scholastic printing, March 1993

For Brittany, Delia, Erin, and Phoebe

contents

Pet-sitters
Plus Five

1

Fire!

"Is everybody listening?" asked Ida Rose. "I'm about to make an important announcement."

Everybody was: Ida, Missy Mason, Betsy Jones, and Betsy's cat, Marbles.

It was a boring summer day, and they were all sitting in Betsy's backyard.

"Of course we're listening," said Missy. "How can we help it? You're so LOUD!"

"You better not be rude to me, Missy," said Ida. "I might not let you join."

"Join what, for Petey's sake?" said Missy.

"That's what I'm trying to tell you, if you could be quiet for two seconds!" yelled Ida.

Betsy watched an ant crawl through the grass. It was carrying a crumb about ten times bigger than itself. Amazing.

Marbles watched it, too. Then he went back to sleep.

Betsy rubbed her cat's head. She wished Missy and Ida wouldn't start fighting.

Whenever they did, she got stuck in the middle.

"Come on, Ida," she said. "Tell us."

"All right." Ida stood up. She tossed her long, beautiful hair. She cleared her throat. "Here is my announcement. The three of us are . . ."

"I smell smoke," said Missy.

"You do not!" cried Ida. "You just want to interrupt me again!"

"I really do," said Missy. "Don't you, Bets?"

"No," said Betsy.

"Your nose is too long. That's your problem," said Ida.

Missy clapped both hands over her nose. It *was* very long. Not to mention skinny. Kind of a Pinocchio nose.

"Don't you dare make fun of my nose," she said. She sounded like she had a head cold. Or like she was a Martian. "I never make fun of you being fat."

"I'm not fat!" said Ida.

"You're definitely not skinny."

"Well, your hair sticks up like crabgrass."

"Can you please not fight?" said Betsy.

Missy lay back on the grass, her hands still hiding her nose.

"Bugs are going to crawl all over you," said Ida.

"Ida, what's your announcement?" asked Betsy.

Ida took a deep breath. "The announcement is: we're starting a club."

"I hate clubs," said Missy in her space alien voice.

"What kind of club?" asked Betsy.

"It's called the ABC. It stands for Animal Baby-sitters Club. I'm the president, you're the vice president, and Crabby over there is treasurer."

"Figures *you're* the president," said Missy. But she looked half-interested.

"What do you mean, animal baby-sitters?" asked Betsy.

She felt excited. Betsy loved anything with more than two legs.

"We baby-sit pets for people who go away," said Ida. "Look at this."

She reached into her backpack and pulled out a pile of papers.

"My mother ran them off for me at her office."

Betsy took one and read:

Animal Babysitters Club
PRESIDENT IDA ROSE

We take care of :
cats
dogs (only friendly)
turtles
birds
fish
hamsters and gerbils
NO RATS, MICE OR SNAKES

Vice President : Betsy Jones
Treasurer : Missy Mason
IT'S NO SWEAT * * GREAT CARE FOR YOUR PET

Call us today at 231-5678

"We'll give these out to all our neighbors," said Ida. "I bet we'll get a ton of business."

"It's a great idea!" said Betsy. "I always wanted more pets. No offense, Marbles." She gave her cat a hug.

"Plus," said Ida, "we might make some money. If we do a really good job, people might pay us."

"I'll do it for free!"

Missy sat up, her hands still over her nose.

"I bet nobody will call us," she said, in that space alien voice.

"Maybe they will!" said Betsy.

"Besides," said Missy, "you can forget me. My mother won't let me bring any pets in the house. Not with Teddy Smeddy crying all day."

"Your brother's still teething?" said Ida. "He must be part vampire."

"Not even a real little one?" asked Betsy. "Like a hamster or a fish?"

Missy shook her head. She took her hands off her nose.

"Are you guys sure you don't smell smoke?"

"Hey," said Betsy, "I think you're right."

"I don't smell a thing," said Ida. "Now listen. I'm the president, so . . ."

Just then they heard a siren.

Betsy's big sister, Julia, came running out the back door.

"Fire!" she cried. "Down on Coventry! Come on!"

2

The Rescue

Coventry Road was two blocks away. They were still one block away when they felt the heat.

"Keep back! Keep back!"

Firefighters and police were everywhere. A yellow tape blocked off the street. Betsy, Ida, Missy, and Julia stood on a corner. Yellow-gray smoke rolled up from the roof of the building.

"I told you I smelled smoke," said Missy.

"This is terrible," said Betsy.

Downstairs, the building was a gift shop and drugstore. Upstairs, it was apartments.

More fire trucks came screaming up. Ladders rose. Water jetted from huge hoses. Suddenly, angry-looking flames shot out of the roof.

"What if somebody's still inside?" cried Betsy.

"They're looking," said Julia. "Don't worry!"

A firefighter smashed the shop windows with his axe. Smoke came pouring out.

"I was just in there yesterday!" said Ida. "My mother sent me for milk!"

Betsy's eyes were stinging. Partly from the smoke. Partly from wanting to cry.

Just then, a firefighter in a yellow coat and monsterlike mask leaned out of an upstairs window. He had something small in his hands. Down below, another firefighter rushed over and caught it.

For a moment, he stared down at his hands. Then they saw him smile. He

looked around, and came straight toward them.

"Can you girls take care of something for me?"

Betsy gasped. It was a tiny gray kitten.

"Mew!" it wailed, opening its pink mouth as wide as it could. "Mew!"

Betsy started to reach for it, but Ida stepped up.

"I'll take it," she said.

"Meow!" yowled the kitten as she grabbed it. "Mew mew mew!" It started to dig into her with its needlelike claws.

"Yikes!" said Ida. "Here, Betsy." She held it out.

Betsy took it gently. The kitten tucked its head under her arm. She could feel its tiny heart pounding. Around its neck was a strange, rainbow-colored collar.

"Great!" said the firefighter, and hurried away.

The fire seemed to be getting bigger instead of smaller. Finally a police officer came and told them they'd have to leave.

"We're clearing the area," she said.

"But . . ." *But what about the kitten? What if the owner comes looking?* Betsy meant to say.

The police officer cut her off with a stern look.

"Come on," said Julia.

They started toward home.

"Mew," said the kitten loudly.

"Wow," said Ida. "I didn't think we'd get our first ABC customer this quick!"

3

First Customer

Julia was downstairs, calling all her friends about the fire.

Betsy, Missy, and Ida took the kitten up to Betsy's room. They put it on her bed.

"I bet it's exhausted," said Betsy. "It probably wants a nap."

Instead, the kitten started to climb up her curtains.

"What do you think you're doing?" laughed Betsy.

"It's loco," said Ida.

"All kittens are like that," said Betsy. "Look at its beautiful collar. It's like all different color threads, twisted together."

The kitten pounced on Ida's hand.

"It's loco!" cried Ida, jumping up.

"It probably thinks you're a nice plump mouse," said Missy. "I'll get it some food."

She came back with a little dish of cat food. Betsy's cat, Marbles, followed her.

"Here you go," said Missy. She put the dish on the bed.

The kitten put both paws in the dish. The whole thing flipped over. Cat food went flying.

"I told you it's loco," said Ida.

"Hissssssss!"

They all turned around. Marbles' back was arched. His tail was a giant puffball. He looked like a Halloween cat.

"Hisss!" he said again, showing his teeth.

The little kitten looked very interested. It went to the edge of the bed and looked down at Marbles.

"Hisss!" it said back, in its baby voice.

And then it leaped straight onto Marbles' back.

"Yeow!"

"Mew!"

"Cat fight!" yelled Ida. "I'm out of here!"

She ran out of the room.

The two cats rolled across the floor, scratching and howling. They crashed into Betsy's desk, knocking off her rock collection.

"Marbles, no!" cried Betsy. "It's just a baby! Marbles, no!"

Marbles didn't pay any attention. The kitten ran under the bed, and Marbles dashed after it.

"We've got to stop them!" said Betsy. "The kitten's going to get creamed!" She reached under the bed.

"Don't!" said Ida from the doorway. "They'll tear you to pieces!"

"Hold on," said Missy. She ran out of the room, and came back with a big glass of water. She stood by the bed. She looked like the Statue of Liberty, holding a glass instead of a torch.

The cats ran out. Missy dumped the whole glass on top of them.

"Yow!" screeched both cats together. They froze and looked at each other in amazement.

Betsy swooped the kitten up. Missy grabbed Marbles.

"Bad boy!" said Missy.

"Poor thing!" said Betsy.

"Is the coast clear?" asked Ida from the doorway.

"Come back in, oh fearless president," said Missy.

Ida folded her arms across her chest. "Don't make fun of me, Missy Mason." She looked around the room. "Look at this place. It's a disaster area."

The rug was wet. Cat food was all over. The floor was a rocky road.

"Good thing Mom's at work," said Betsy.

"First we'll clean up," said Ida. "Then we'll hand out our fliers to the neighbors."

The kitten came along, peeking its head over Betsy's shoulder just like a baby.

"If it was mine, I'd name it Princess," said Betsy.

"Or Thumbelina," said Missy. "It's so teeny."

"There's no sense naming it," said Ida, as she stuck a flier in a door. "We're not keeping it."

"I *know*," said Betsy.

Ida looked at her. "Don't tell me *you're* getting cranky now, too!"

When Betsy's mother, Mrs. Jones, got

home, they told her the whole story.

"Poor little thing," said Mrs. Jones. She took the kitten from Betsy. "What an unusual collar. Somebody made this by hand. Somebody really loves you, don't they?" She gave the kitten back to Betsy. "Let's go find the owner."

The fire was finally out. The building's front was all black. The windows were broken, and the roof was caved in.

Betsy hugged the kitten tight.

The firefighters were gone. But the police were still there. Mrs. Jones told one of them about the kitten.

The policeman shook his head. "Nobody's come looking for a cat," he said.

"Do you know where the people who lived here are staying?" asked Mrs. Jones.

"All over," he said. "Some went with relatives. Some are at a shelter." He shook his head again. "Nobody's going to stay in those apartments, that's for sure. Not for a long time."

"Thank you," said Mrs. Jones.

Nobody said anything as they started home. The smell of smoke was still heavy in the air.

Then Ida said, "We can put up some posters that say, DID YOU LOSE A KITTEN?"

"That's a good idea, Ida," said Mrs. Jones.

"If nobody claims it, we get to keep it," said Missy. "Right?"

"*You* can't keep it," said Ida. "Your mother won't let you, because of Teddy."

Missy pulled down her eyes and pushed up her nose. She looked like a seasick pig. "Teddy Smeddy," she said.

"And my mother's allergic to cats," said Ida. "She won't let me, either."

Betsy's heart skipped a beat.

"Then that means . . ." She looked at her mother.

"You can keep it tonight," said Mrs.

Jones. "But I'm sure the owner will claim it by tomorrow."

Betsy held the kitten tight. Its little gray head rubbed under her chin. Its fur was the softest thing she'd ever felt.

4

In Good Hands

Next morning Betsy was pouring the kitten a little bowl of milk when the phone rang.

"Important club meeting," said Ida. "N-o-w!"

Betsy took the kitten with her.

Ida lived right next door. She was out on her front porch, surrounded by paper.

"I got up at 7:08 to make them," said Ida. "I figured it was the president's duty."

The posters said:

RESCUED: ONE GRAY KITTEN!
FROM THE BIG FIRE!

DON'T WORRY! IT'S IN GOOD HANDS: THE ANIMAL
BABY-SITTERS CLUB
IF IT IS YOURS, CALL PRESIDENT IDA ROSE
AT 231-5678

Betsy could tell there wasn't one mistake. Ida was excellent at spelling.

"You made the letters nice and big," she said.

Ida smiled proudly. "Nobody will be able to miss them."

"That's what I'm afraid of."

"What?" said Ida.

23

"Nothing," said Betsy.

She tried to hug the kitten, but it jumped down from her arms. It walked straight across the posters.

"Loco," said Ida.

"It slept on my bed last night," said Betsy. "Sort of slept. Mostly it kept jumping on my head. I had to keep the door shut, so Marbles wouldn't come in. He sat outside and meowed." She yawned. "I didn't get much sleep."

"Your troubles will be over when the owner reads this." Ida tapped a poster. "Oooh, a spider!" She jumped up and stamped it with her shoe.

Missy came over. She read the posters.

"You don't say if it's a boy or girl cat," she said.

"Because we don't know!" said Ida.

"All you have to do is look," said Missy.

"Not me," said Ida.

Betsy just giggled.

"Oh for Petey's sake," said Missy. She

picked up the kitten and flipped it over. "Boy," she said.

Ida changed the posters to read: RESCUED: ONE GRAY MALE KITTEN!

"We should name him Lucky Boy," said Missy.

"I was thinking of Smoky," said Betsy.

"There's no sense naming it. We're not keeping it," said Ida. "Come on. We have to hang these up."

All the storekeepers let them put their posters in the store windows. But nobody knew who the kitten belonged to.

"That collar . . . it looks familiar," said the woman in Coventry Pizza. "Maybe . . . No, I just can't say."

The windows of the burned-out building were all boarded up now.

"It's a real disaster," said Missy. "I saw it on the news last night."

Betsy held the kitten close as they hurried by.

Back at Ida's, the phone was ringing.

"Hello?" Ida said. "Yes, this is the ABC president."

Her voice got more and more excited.

"It's not on our list, but that's okay . . . Today? We'll be right over."

She hung up.

"Wow, this club was a brilliant idea."

"What kind of pet is it?"

"A cricket," said Ida.

"A cricket!" said Missy. "We have to take care of a *bug*?"

5

Different People Love Different Things

"It's not a bug," said Ida. "It's Ben Copper's pet cricket. Let's go."

At the Coppers' house, Ben was sitting on the front steps, a small cage on his lap.

"Here it is," he said. Inside the cage, something big, black, and hairy jumped around.

"Yuck!" said Ida, stepping back.

Ben Copper frowned. "Are you saying yuck to my cricket?"

"Don't mind her," said Missy. "Give it to me."

She took the cage. A tiny bell hung from its top. The cricket hopped up and rang it.

"A trained bug!" cried Missy. "Fantastic!"

"His name is Chirpy," said Ben. "Here's a bag of the bark and leaves he eats. The liverwurst is for a special treat. That little sponge has to stay wet. That's his water."

"It's no sweat—great care for your pet," said Ida.

Ben put his face close to the cage.

"Goodbye, Chirpy," he said softly. "I'll miss you."

"He's in good hands," said Ida.

"I sure hope so," said Ben. "I'll see you in three days."

Back at Ida's house, they put the cricket and the kitten down on the porch.

Pounce! The kitten jumped on top of the cage. Swipe! He tried to stick his paw in.

"Cut that out!" yelled Betsy. She grabbed the kitten. "You're not a lion," she told him. "Stop attacking everything!"

He jumped out of her arms. Pounce! He was back on top of the cage.

"I said cut that out!"

"Forget it," said Ida. "Cats don't obey you. They just do what they want. Who'd ever want a cat for a pet?"

Missy picked up the cricket cage. Ding! It rang its bell.

"This is the pet for me," she said. "A trained bug. Fantastic."

"Ugh and yuck!" said Ida. "That hairy, gross thing? How could anyone love a *bug*?"

"Different people love different things," said Missy.

Ida made them tomato sandwiches and chocolate milk for lunch. They took the phone outside with them, in case they got any more calls.

And sure enough, they did.

6

Haar Haar Haar!

"Yes, this is President Ida Rose. Oh, hi, Mrs. Wells . . . What? I mean, excuse me? . . . Yes . . . Of course we can! We'll be right over!"

She hung up.

"That was Mrs. Wells. They have a family emergency and have to go to Columbus overnight. They can't find a kennel to take their dog!"

"That's not a dog," said Missy. "It's a horse."

"For your information, it's a Newfound-land. It eats tons, and needs loads of exercise. It's a HUGE responsibility. I told them of course the ABC could handle it."

"This is just great," said Missy. "First the kitten's going to eat the cricket. Then Marbles is going to eat the kitten. And then that humungous dog is going to eat Marbles!"

"I don't know why you're even in this club, Missy Mason!" said Ida. "All you do is whine."

"And all you do is boss," said Missy.

"No I don't!"

"Yes you do. Doesn't she, Bets?"

"At least I'm not the sourest person in the world, like you. Right, Betsy?"

Betsy picked up the kitten.

"You know why I like animals so much?" she said. "Because they don't argue and make me be in the middle."

Ida tossed her hair.

"Anyway," she said, "the dog stays at the Wellses' house. We just feed it and walk it."

"I hope he comes with a saddle," said Missy.

Ida made a face at her. "I told her we'd be right over."

"I better leave you here," Betsy told the kitten. "Don't worry. I'll be back soon!"

The Wellses lived only two houses away, on the other side of Betsy's house. Mrs. Wells was on the front lawn. An enormous dog sat beside her.

"Thank you for doing this on such short notice," said Mrs. Wells. "I don't know what we'd have done. Baby's really too big to travel with."

"Haaaar!" barked Baby.

His tongue was half as long as Betsy's arm. His teeth reminded her of pocket knives.

"Our ad . . ." Ida's voice was a tiny squeak. "Our ad said only friendly dogs."

"Oh my," said Mrs. Wells. "Baby's as friendly as they come! Aren't you, Baby?"

"Haaar haaar haaar!"

"The only time he's unfriendly is if he's hungry. Be sure to feed him tonight. The bag of food is under the sink, in the kitchen."

She took a key from her purse and handed it to Ida. Then she held out Baby's leash.

"A walk right now would be a good idea. Get to know each other."

Ida stared at the leash as if it were the fuse to a firecracker.

Mr. Wells was backing the car down the driveway. Mrs. Wells put the leash in Ida's hand.

"No pet—great care for your sweat," she squeaked. "I mean . . ."

"Thank you again, girls. We appreciate

this so much. We should be home by tomorrow evening. Baby, you be good." She kissed the dog on the nose. "Good-bye!"

The car pulled away.

"Haaar haaaar haaaar!" bellowed Baby.

Then he washed Ida's face with his tongue.

"Oooh! Ugh! Quit it!" said Ida.

Baby shut his mouth. He flattened himself at her feet.

"How do you like that?" said Ida. "Finally, an animal that does what you tell it. Sit, Baby."

The dog sat up.

"Lie down."

Baby went flat.

"This is my kind of pet!" said Ida. "Let's go for a walk, Baby."

They took a long walk. Ida wouldn't let Betsy hold the leash.

"He's used to me now," she said. "Quit that, Baby," she said, as Baby stopped to smell something disgusting-looking. "And don't even think about barking at that squirrel."

Back at the Wellses' house, Ida unlocked the door and took Baby in. When she came back out, she was smiling proudly.

"This club may be the best idea I ever had," she said, "and I've had millions of good ideas."

"Give us a break," said Missy, making her seasick pig face.

"Let's get back to your house," said Betsy. "I want to make sure my—I mean the—kitten's okay."

7

Little Angel

The kitten was sound asleep in the clothes basket. He looked just like a kitten on a calendar. Betsy longed to pick him up.

But she didn't. She knew kittens needed their rest, just like babies.

"I can't believe nobody's claimed you yet," she whispered. The tiny gray ear twitched. "If you were mine, I'd be going crazy trying to find you!"

The phone rang.

Ida's voice sounded excited.

"For Petey's sake," said Missy. "Don't tell me it's *another* job!"

Betsy held her breath.

Maybe, finally, it was the kitten's owner.

Ida hung up.

"A hamster! This time it's a hamster!"

Her shout woke the kitten up. He gave a huge yawn. Betsy scooped him up and held him close.

"Zoe Lustic is going to camp, and her mother is scared to touch it. We get it for two whole weeks!"

Zoe brought the hamster over in her wagon.

"These wood chips go in the bottom of the cage," she said, "and this cotton goes in her little house. Here's her food."

"What are all those little black things?" asked Missy.

"That's her . . . you know," said Zoe. "I didn't get around to cleaning the cage."

Missy pretended to faint.

"Please take her out and play with her," said Zoe. "She'll get real lonesome if you don't."

"It's no sweat—great care for your pet," said Ida.

"Goodbye, Little Angel," Zoe said. "I'll see you in two weeks!"

By now it was almost supper time. Betsy's mother called for her to come home.

"We'll help you carry all the cages," said Ida.

"What do you mean?" said Betsy. "I already have the kitten!"

"Missy's mother will never let her bring a bug or a rodent home," said Ida. "She's too afraid of Teddy getting germs."

"It's true," said Missy sadly.

"And my mother's allergic to crickets and hamsters," said Ida.

"You said she was allergic to cats!"

Ida tossed her hair. "She's allergic to lots of stuff."

Betsy looked around at the pouncing

kitten, hopping cricket, and stinky hamster. She tried to imagine taking care of them all herself.

"I know," she said. "I'll ask my mother if I can have a sleep-over. Then we can all take care of them!"

"Fantastic!" yelled Missy.

"Let's go!" cried Ida.

"Why not?" said Mrs. Jones. "If I'm going to have a house full of critters, I might as well throw in a couple of extra kids, too."

8

Everything's Ruined!

They put Marbles outside.

They put the cricket in the extra bedroom, with the door shut tight.

They couldn't find the kitten.

"He's probably curled up asleep somewhere," said Betsy. "This is a good time to clean Little Angel's cage."

"I'm glad we already ate," said Missy, "or I'd lose my appetite."

"How come you think this is so gross, but you love that hairy cricket?" Ida asked her.

"I told you," said Missy. "People are different."

"You're different all right," said Ida.

"No fighting at my sleep-over!" said Betsy.

They dumped out the cage, and put in fresh wood chips and cotton. They carried it up to Betsy's room, and took Little Angel out to play.

"Sit in a circle," said Ida. "Spread your legs out. That way she can't get away from us."

The hamster scurried around among them.

"Look how flat she can make herself," said Ida. "It's like her bones bend or something."

"She's so soft," said Betsy. "I love her little black eyes."

"As long as she doesn't, you know, on the rug," said Missy.

"Would you quit talking about that?" said Ida.

Then she gave a scream.

"Yeow! What was that? Something attacked me!" She jumped up, and hopped on one foot. "Yeow!"

The kitten flew out from under the bed and pounced on her other foot.

"So that's where you were, you little devil!" said Betsy. She dove after the kitten.

"Wait a second!" said Missy. "Where's the hamster?"

"What?"

"Oh no! Hurry up! Find her!"

"How could she get away so fast?"

They looked under the bed. In the closet. In the pile of clothes Betsy kept forgetting to hang up. Under her desk and in her desk. Under her dresser and in her dresser.

"She's no place!" wailed Missy.

"Don't be ridiculous," said Ida. "She can't just disappear!"

"Remember how flat she could make

herself?" said Betsy. "She could have squeezed in anywhere."

"It's that loco kitten's fault," said Ida. "Little Angel saw him, and she ran for her life."

"The kitten couldn't help it," said Betsy. "Hunting is a cat instinct."

"We'll have to search the whole house," said Ida. "Everybody spread out."

Betsy was taking all the food out of the kitchen cupboard when her mother came in.

"What on earth are you doing?"

Betsy hated to tell her.

The club had been going so well.

She'd been so proud of how they were handling everything.

Now it was all ruined. Nobody would ever trust them with a pet again.

"Mom, we . . . we . . ."

"Don't tell me you lost that hamster."

Betsy nodded miserably.

"Show me where you had it last."

Betsy took her mother upstairs. Missy was throwing all the towels out of the hall closet. Ida was going through the dirty clothes hamper.

"In my room," said Betsy.

Mrs. Jones looked around. Then she said, "You girls might as well give up."

"Give up!" cried Ida. "We'll never give up!"

"I'm afraid that little critter got into the wall. Through the heat grate." She pointed to it.

"In the wall!" said Betsy. "But . . ."

"At least it's not winter," said Mrs. Jones. "The heat's not on. If it was, we'd have fried hamster."

"Mom!" Betsy started to cry.

That set Missy off, too. Ida never cried. But her lip trembled.

"It's getting late," said Mrs. Jones. "Time for the Animal Baby-sitters Club to go to bed."

"But we can't! We can't!"

"When it gets hungry, the hamster might come out by itself. If it doesn't, you can look some more tomorrow."

"Everything's ruined," said Betsy. "Our whole club is wrecked."

9

Did We Forget Something?

Nobody could get to sleep.

They lay in their sleeping bags on Betsy's floor.

The kitten kept pouncing on them.

Ida kept swatting it away.

Betsy kept protecting it.

Missy kept sniffling about the hamster.

Ida kept telling her not to act like a baby.

Betsy kept asking them not to fight.

Then the cricket started to chirp.

They couldn't believe how loud it sounded.

"Cree, cree, creeeeeeeeee!"

"It sounds like it's hooked up to its own amplifier," said Missy.

Betsy's big sister, Julia, poked her head in the door. "I can't sleep with that racket," she said. "You've got to get that bug out of here."

"Let's put it down in the basement," said Ida.

The three of them went down together. Betsy's basement was the creepy kind. Especially at night.

"Good night, Chirpy," said Missy. "I like your song, even if no one else does."

Upstairs, they crawled back into their sleeping bags.

"I hope Chirpy's all right," said Missy. "I hope some giant spider doesn't attack him. Do you think spiders eat crickets?"

"Listen," said Betsy. "I can hear him all the way up here."

52

They listened. Sure enough, they could hear, very faintly, the "Cree cree creeeee!"

"Amazing," said Betsy.

"Can you believe they do that by rubbing their wings together?" said Missy.

"Wait a second," said Ida. She sat up straight. "I think I hear something else."

They all listened.

"Haaar haaaar haaaaar!"

It sounded like a sea lion the size of King Kong.

Or someone throwing metal garbage cans around inside a tunnel.

"Baby!" Ida leaped up. "We forgot to feed Baby!"

Missy put her head under her pillow. "I'm resigning from this club," she said. "Right now."

"Oh no you're not," said Betsy. She pulled Missy up. "Come on! And be quiet! I don't want my mother to know we messed up on the dog, too!"

10

In the Wet, Dark Night

It was starting to rain.

"Careful you don't step on a slug," Missy told Ida.

"Sssssh!" said Betsy. "The neighbors will hear you!"

Baby was barking his head off by now.

"He sounds like he's starving," said Missy. "I wouldn't go in there for anything. Remember what Mrs. Wells said about how unfriendly he gets? If it moves, he'll eat it!"

Ida stood very still. She looked as if, finally, she was going to bash Missy in the nose.

"This just goes to show why I'm president and you're not, Missy Mason," she said. "Presidents know how to take responsibility. People can count on them. Oh no."

Even in the dim light, Betsy could see Ida turn pale.

"Oh no," she said again.

"What?" asked Betsy. "What's the matter?"

"The key," said Ida weakly. "I left it in the house."

"You mean we're locked out?"

Ida nodded.

"Fantastic," said Missy. "We're locked out in the pouring rain, the hamster is in the wall, and the big Baby is going to starve to death."

That was when Ida burst into tears.

Betsy and Missy couldn't believe it.

Ida never, ever cried.

"I'm sorry," said Missy. "I didn't mean . . ."

"Oh shut up," sobbed Ida.

"Haaar haaaar haaaaar!" barked Baby, louder than ever.

Betsy put an arm around Ida.

Missy disappeared into the darkness.

"Where's she going?" sobbed Ida.

"I don't know," said Betsy.

"I hope she went home! I hope I never see her again!"

"This isn't her fault," said Betsy.

"I know!" said Ida. She shook off Betsy's arm. "It's all *my* fault!"

"I didn't mean that," said Betsy. "I just meant . . ."

"I found one!" Missy came running back to them.

"One what?"

"An open window! I can get in! Come on!"

They followed her around to the side of the house.

"I'll need a boost," said Missy.

"Wait a minute," said Betsy. "What if Baby thinks you're a robber? He might attack you."

"Just a second," said Missy. She disappeared again.

This time she came back waving a hamburger left over from their supper.

"I heard that this is how robbers make friends with dogs," she said. "Okay. Boost me up."

"But you're really scared of Baby."

"I know! Hurry up before I chicken out!"

"Wait a minute," said Ida. "I'm the president. I'm going with you. Betsy, you be the lookout."

They boosted Ida in first.

Then Missy climbed in the window.

Baby's barking stopped immediately.

Did that mean he was licking their faces?
Or chomping them both down?

In the wet, dark night, Betsy waited.

Then she saw headlights coming down the street.

A police car!

Maybe a neighbor had called about the noise! That was all they needed now—the entire ABC arrested!

She dove under a bush.

Headlights swept across the grass. She squeezed her eyes shut.

"For Petey's sake, what are you doing under the bushes?"

Betsy jumped up. Ida, Missy, and Baby stood in front of her.

They were all grinning. The police car was nowhere in sight.

"He didn't eat you!"

"Everything's fine. We just brought him out so he could do his—you know," said Missy.

"And this time," said Ida, "I have the key!" She held it up.

"Haar haar haar!" barked Baby, and washed her face.

"Will you quit that?" said Ida happily.

11

No Sweat

It was a miracle. They got back into the house without waking up Mr. and Mrs. Jones or Julia.

They let Marbles, who was wet and very sad, in the house. They shut the bedroom door before he could get in.

The girls changed back into their pajamas. Then they crawled back into their sleeping bags.

The kitten snuggled down beside Betsy. She stroked his head. She had never been so tired in her life.

"Uh-oh," said Missy.

Betsy's eyes flew open. "Now what?"

"Chirpy. I don't hear him."

They all listened. Except for Marbles scratching at the bedroom door, all was silence.

"We've got to go down and check on him," said Missy.

Betsy and Ida both lay very still.

The last thing Betsy wanted to do was go down into her creepy basement this time of night.

She knew Ida felt exactly the same way.

"Maybe Chirpy's just asleep," Betsy suggested.

Missy jumped up. "Crickets chirp at night! I'm going down. If no one else wants to come, I'll go myself."

"Oh, no you don't," said Ida, jumping up, too. "You helped me with Baby, so I should . . ." She stopped, blushed, and kicked a pillow. "Anyway, I'm the president. It's my responsibility. Let's go, Miss!"

"Wait for me!" Betsy grabbed the kitten, and together they tiptoed out into the hall.

"Meow!" said Marbles when he saw them.

"Sssh!"

"Ssssh!"

"Sssssh!"

Down in the basement, Chirpy was silently nibbling on his liverwurst.

"Good boy, Chirpy!" said Missy. She blew the cricket a kiss.

For once the kitten didn't try to attack the bug. Instead he stayed very still in Betsy's arms, green eyes wide.

It's almost like he knows this is important, thought Betsy. *Amazing.*

"Good kitty," she whispered.

The kitten's tail gave a sudden twitch. She felt his muscles tense up.

She looked where he was looking.

In a dark corner, something moved.

"Missy! Ida!" she whispered. "Look!"

"The hamster!" whispered Missy. She started toward it.

"Wait!" Ida picked up an empty paint can. "Let's try to bump him into this." Missy grabbed an old piece of screen.

"Great. You knock him in, and I'll whip this on top."

Betsy held the kitten. She also held her breath.

"Got him!" yelled Missy and Ida together.

"All right!" shouted Betsy. She kissed the kitten three times in a row. "Hurray!"

The ABC started up the stairs. Mrs. Jones stood at the top.

"It's 2 A.M. What in the world do you think you're doing?"

"It's no sweat! Great care for your pet!" said Betsy.

All three of them nearly fell back down the stairs laughing.

12

The True Owner

Betsy was so tired, even the kitten couldn't wake her up.

Every time he jumped on her head, she pushed him away and went back to her dream.

She dreamed the kitten's owner came. It was a very tall man, dressed like a magician.

He looked at Chirpy, Baby, and Little Angel, all sitting in a row.

He said, "You have taken such good

care of them all, I will grant you one wish."

Betsy said, "I wish I could keep the kitten."

The man nodded. "No sweat," he said, and disappeared.

Betsy opened her eyes.

Missy and Ida were still asleep.

Marbles was lying at the bottom of her sleeping bag.

I forgot to shut the door last night, thought Betsy. *Why didn't he and the kitten fight?*

The kitten walked over to Marbles and gave him a swat.

Marbles just blinked.

"Poor Marbs," said Betsy. "You're so glad to be allowed in here, you're not even going to fight."

"What? What'd you say?" Missy sat up with a yawn.

Her hair was sticking up in about ten different directions.

Ida rolled over with a groan. "What a night," she said.

"But everything turned out great," said Betsy. She reached for the kitten, and rubbed him under his beautiful collar.

"I never knew taking care of things was such hard work," said Missy.

Just then Julia came in.

"Ida, your mother said to come home— you have an important phone call."

"It must be another job!"

Ida threw on her clothes and ran out the door.

"Great," said Missy, as she and Betsy started to clean up the room. "What will it be next? A pet piranha?"

The kitten kept jumping on the sleeping bag strings.

"I was thinking," said Betsy. "Magic might be a good name."

"You really love that kitten, don't you, Bets?"

Just then Ida came back in.

Betsy could tell right away the phone call wasn't another job.

Ida didn't toss her hair, grin, or shout.

Instead, she looked at Betsy as if she wished she didn't have to say what she had to say.

Betsy scooped up the kitten and held him close.

"I know," she whispered. "The owner."

Ida nodded. "It's meeting us on Coventry in half an hour."

13

Schnickelfritz

"*It?*" cried Missy. "The owner's an *it?*"

"I couldn't tell if it was a man or a woman," said Ida. "The voice was so old and shaky."

Betsy's feet felt as if they had boulders attached. The walk to Coventry seemed to take ten years.

The kitten looked over her shoulder, just like a baby. His needlelike little claws dug into her. His silky gray ears turned this way and that.

Betsy's throat felt so tight, she could hardly swallow.

"It's a woman," said Ida. "There, on the bench."

A very, very old woman sat on a bench near the burned-out building. A woman about the age of Mrs. Jones sat beside her. The old woman stood up when she saw them.

"Schnickelfritz!" she exclaimed, in a creaky voice.

"What did she say?" whispered Ida.

"My little Schnickelfritz!" said the old woman. She reached two small, wrinkled hands toward the kitten, then let them drop.

"Is *that* the kitten's name?" asked Betsy.

The old woman gave a chuckle. "He was such a mischief! Such a little clown!"

She's right, thought Betsy. *It's the perfect name for him.*

The younger woman stood up now.

"So you're the three heroines who saved my mother's cat! I can't thank you enough."

Ida tossed her hair. "We were glad to do it," she said.

"My mother was visiting me the day of the fire," said the woman. "Thank goodness. I don't know if she'd have made it down the stairs in time!"

The old woman's eyes filled with tears. She sat back down.

"She lost everything," said the daughter.

They all looked at the boarded-up building. Betsy remembered how the flames had shot out the roof.

"We thought the kitten was gone, too," said the daughter. "My mother was beside herself. Then I saw your signs."

"I was so happy," whispered the old woman.

"Where . . . where will you live?" Betsy asked.

74

She started to answer, but the daughter interrupted.

"With me, of course. I've wanted her to come live with me for a long time. Now she has no choice!"

The old woman shook her head.

For the first time, Betsy noticed the edges of her blouse were stitched with the same rainbow-colored threads as the kitten's collar.

She made it for him, Betsy thought. With those wrinkly old hands.

The old woman leaned toward Betsy.

"My daughter has a very fancy house," she said in her soft, rusty voice. "Too fancy for a kitten."

Betsy's heart skipped a beat.

"Mother!" said the daughter. "What are you talking about? I told you you could keep the cat!"

The old woman shook her head. "Too fancy for a cat. Cat hair on the nice sofa. Scratching on the nice dining room chairs.

Digging up the flower beds." She reached up and stroked the kitten between the ears. "Too fancy for a Schnickelfritz."

"You mean we can keep it?" asked Missy.

The old woman, her eyes glistening, said, "I know you'll take good care of him."

Missy gave Betsy a hug.

But Ida said, "Why'd you call us up, if you don't want the kitten back?"

The woman reached out and stroked Ida's head, just the way she'd stroked the kitten.

"I had to thank you," she said. "Such nice little girls."

The old woman stood up. She swayed a little, and her daughter caught her elbow.

"Such nice little girls," repeated the old woman. "You'll take good care of my little boy."

"For all you've done," said the daughter, and she handed Ida a $5 bill. "I have

to get my mother home now. I can see she needs a rest."

"Here!" Betsy pressed Schnickelfritz into the old woman's arms. "Take him! You lost everything else. He'll cheer you up."

The old woman looked surprised. Then, she folded the kitten close.

"I thought I had to give up everything now," she said. "But . . . but maybe not." Eyes wet, she gave Betsy a slow smile.

"I wish you'd make up your mind!" said the daughter. "First you . . . yow!"

She jumped as the kitten swiped her bare arm.

"Schnickelfritz!" said the old woman sternly.

But Betsy saw the twinkle in her old eyes.

"Goodbye!" said the daughter, and marched her mother down the street.

"Five divided by three," said Ida.

"That's . . . a dollar sixty something each."

"I never saw so many wrinkles," said Missy.

Betsy couldn't say anything. She was trying to keep the kitten in sight as long as she could.

14

The Amazing ABC

They started home. Ida stopped to push a worm out of a puddle with her shoe.

"You're saving a worm?" said Missy. "For Petey's sake—you hate bugs!"

Ida tossed her hair. "Once you start taking care of things, it's hard to stop," she said. "Anyway, we better go back to my house. In case we get any more jobs."

"All right," said Missy.

But Betsy wanted to be alone for a while.

"I'm going home," she said.

Up in her room, Marbles was stretched out on the bed. When Betsy came in, he stood up, ready to jump.

"I'm not going to throw you out," said Betsy softly. "Don't worry. The kitten's gone."

She pulled Marbles onto her lap and petted him. It had been two whole days since she'd done that.

Marbles purred.

"She was really glad to get her kitten back," Betsy told him.

Marbles kept on purring.

"She was so nice. And her daughter was so bossy. Missy's right. People are really different."

Marbles purred away.

He wasn't as much fun as a kitten. Or as adorable.

But he was a much better listener.

Betsy began to feel a little bit better.

"Surprise!" Missy and Ida burst into the room. Ida was waving a big piece of paper.

It said, in perfect, neat handwriting:

Roses are red.
Violets are blue.
Kittens are sweet.
And so are you!

Underneath was a very messy drawing of a gray kitten.

"I did the writing," said Ida. "Missy drew the picture."

"We cooperated," explained Missy.

"Amazing!" said Betsy. "I'm going to hang it up by my bed."

Just then they heard a sound.

It was like a sea lion the size of King Kong.

Or someone throwing metal garbage cans around in a tunnel.

"Haaaar haaaar haaaar!"

"Baby! We forgot him again!"

And the ABC ran out the door.

About the Author

Tricia Springstubb's daughter used to have a pet-sitting business, which inspired her mother to write this book. Though there were not nearly as many mishaps, a hamster did create some problems for their family cat, Marbles.

Ms. Springstubb lives in Ohio with her husband, their three daughters, and Marbles. She has written many books for children. She is the author of *Two Plus One Makes Trouble*, another story about Betsy, Ida, and Missy.